D0990775

CAN YOU NAB THE MOTHMAN?

AN INTERACTIVE MONSTER HUNT

BY BLAKE HOENA

CAPSTONE PRESS
a capstone imprint

Published by Capstone Press, an imprint of Capstone.
1710 Roe Crest Drive, North Mankato, Minnesota 56003
capstonepub.com

Library of Congress Cataloging-in-Publication Data
Names: Hoena, B. A., author. Title: Can you nab the Mothman? : an interactive
monster hunt / Blake Hoena.
Description: North Mankato, Minnesota : Capstone Press, an imprint of
Capstone, 2022. | Series: You choose: monster hunter | Includes bibliographical
references and index. | Audience: Ages 8-11. | Audience: Grades 4-6. | Summary:
In the role of a cryptozoologist, the reader will investigate three sightings of the
Mothman in three different locations across the country, and choose how the
investigations will proceed.
Identifiers: LCCN 2022008792 (print) | LCCN 2022008793 (ebook) |
ISBN 9781666336931 (hardcover) | ISBN 9781666336948 (paperback) |
ISBN 9781666336955 (pdf)
Subjects: LCSH: Mothman--Juvenile fiction. | Monsters--Juvenile fiction. |
Cryptozoology--Juvenile fiction. | Plot-your-own stories. | CYAC: Mothman--
Fiction. | Monsters--Fiction. | Cryptozoology--Fiction. | Plot-your-own stories. |
LCGFT: Choose-your-own stories.
Classification: LCC PZ7.H67127 Caj 2022 (print) | LCC PZ7.H67127 (ebook) |
DDC 813.6 [Fic]--dc23/eng/20220225
LC record available at https://lccn.loc.gov/2022008792
LC ebook record available at https://lccn.loc.gov/2022008793

Editorial Credits
Editor: Christopher Harbo; Designer: Sarah Bennett; Media Researcher:
Svetlana Zhurkin; Production Specialist: Katy LaVigne

Image Credits
Associated Press: The Herald-Dispatch Archive, 103; Dreamstime: Jim Roberts,
49, Trekandshoot, 74, Visualistka Nina, 6; Getty Images: 6381380, 12, David
Wall, 61, DenisTangneyJr, 27, Herzstaub, 22; Shutterstock: alexkoral, 37,
Andrew Angelov, 31, buonarrotidesig, 44, ChicagoPhotographer, 57, Daniel
Eskridge, 100, 106 (right), Erick Cervantes, 92, Gregory M. Davis Jr., 105, IfH,
39, iusubov nizami, 106 (left), Jack R Perry Photography, 19, jakkapan, 112
(back), James Andrews1, 52, Kalleeck, 107 (bottom), Kit Leong, 67, L.A. Nature
Graphics, 79, Lario Tus, 107 (top), Real Window Creative, 9, Ronald Rampsch,
88, SimpleB, cover, back cover, 1, Vitaly Valua, 41

TABLE OF CONTENTS

ABOUT YOUR ADVENTURE

YOU are a cryptozoologist who studies legendary creatures all over the world. One day, you receive several text messages detailing sightings of the Mothman in West Virginia, Illinois, and California. With multiple sightings across the country, there's no question you're going on a monster hunt. But will you be able to prove this winged, red-eyed beast really exists?

Chapter One sets the scene. Then you choose which path to read. Follow the directions at the bottom of the page as you read the stories. The decisions you make will change your outcome. After you finish one path, go back and read the others for new perspectives and more adventures.

Turn the page to begin your adventure.

Dense foliage and a good pair of binoculars are essential for a cryptozoologist on the hunt for elusive cryptids.

THE MYSTERIOUS MOTHMAN

You're high up in a tree, scanning the dense forest with your binoculars. There have been numerous Bigfoot sightings in these woods, and you're hoping to get a glimpse of the hairy beast—maybe even snap a photo.

But it's been hours since you climbed up to your hiding spot. You're sore from being wedged into the nook of a tree. You're hungry, cold, and have to pee—badly!

Just be patient, you silently tell yourself. You know this is all part of being a cryptozoologist. It's hard work searching for conclusive evidence that legendary beasts such as the Jersey Devil, Wendigo, and Chupacabra exist.

Turn the page.

As the sun starts to sink below the horizon, you call it quits. All you've seen are some squirrels, lots of birds, and a couple of deer. Nothing to tell people about. Nothing that's going to make you famous as a monster hunter.

Before climbing down, you check your phone. You've received dozens of text messages while up in the tree. One is from your friend Ty. Like you, he's also a cryptozoologist. You've even gone on a few expeditions together.

Have you heard of the Mothman? Ty asks.

Of course you have. Learning about strange creatures is what you do. You've seen pictures posted online of the tall, human-like creature with wings and red, glowing eyes.

Yeah, you reply. *Have u seen it?*

I wish, Ty says. *But . . .*

Downtown Point Pleasant, West Virginia, lines the eastern bank of the Ohio River.

He goes on to tell you about recent sightings near Point Pleasant, West Virginia. That is where the legend of the Mothman began back in the 1960s.

You scroll through your other text messages. You have several more from some of your monster-hunting friends. Gabe claims to have seen the mysterious Jersey Devil. Rita is chasing after the bloodsucking Chupacabra.

Turn the page.

Then you read a text from your friend Jackie in Chicago, Illinois. She's a famous blogger from the Midwest.

The Chicago Mothman is back, she wrote. She also mentions reports of strange noises heard in one of the city's parks, and that several people claim to have seen a large flying creature with red eyes. Sounds like a classic Mothman sighting.

You also have a text from your friend Gino in Los Angeles, California. He's a social media influencer with more than a million followers and another cryptozoologist. He messaged you about some strange sightings in nearby La Crescenta. People have seen a large, dark creature with glowing eyes flying about. Another promising report.

Hmm . . . , you think. *It's strange that three of my friends are reporting claims of the same cryptid in three different spots across the country.*

But Ty, Jackie, and Gino are all people you trust. You've hunted monsters with them before, and you know they are reliable. When they say they've heard about a cryptid sighting, you know it is worth checking out. Now you just need to decide who to join in searching for the fabled Mothman.

To head to Point Pleasant with Ty, turn to page 13.

To check out Chicago with Jackie, turn to page 45.

To visit La Crescenta with Gino, turn to page 75.

In 1966, Point Pleasant became famous as the birthplace of the Mothman legend.

CHAPTER 2

POINT PLEASANT, WEST VIRGINIA

Point Pleasant, a small town in West Virginia, is where the legend of the Mothman began. So what better place to go looking for the mysterious cryptid? You'll also be there with your friend Ty, a skilled monster hunter.

While texting back and forth with him, you've learned that the first Mothman sightings occurred back in the fall of 1966. Perhaps the most famous one was when four people claimed to have been chased by a mysterious winged creature with glowing red eyes. They reported it to the local newspaper. Soon after their story was printed, other folks in West Virginia reported seeing the creature.

Turn the page.

Eventually, news of the Mothman spread beyond the Mountain State. People from Chicago to Los Angeles—and even as far away as Russia—have reported sightings of the mysterious Mothman.

"But it all started right here," Ty reminds you once you meet up with him in Point Pleasant.

"Where was the first sighting?" you ask.

"A place people call the TNT Area," Ty says. "It's a few miles north of Point Pleasant."

He goes on to explain that it was the site of an ammunition factory during World War II.

"It's now a wilderness area," Ty continues. "But there are still these creepy, old buried bunkers that were once used to store explosives."

Sounds like the type of place a monster would hide, you think.

"Sounds like a great place to begin our investigation," you say to Ty.

But then he tells you of another place with a strong link to the cryptid.

"What about the Silver Memorial Bridge?" Ty asks. "It replaced the old Silver Bridge, which collapsed a year after the first Mothman sightings. Some folks believe that the Mothman appeared to warn them about what was about to happen."

Could the Mothman be back to warn of another bridge collapse? you wonder.

To head to the TNT Area, turn to page 16.
To check out the new bridge, turn to page 19.

The old ammunition factory is where the legend of the Mothman began. It sounds like a perfect place for a monster to hide, and a perfect spot to begin your investigation.

You and Ty head north from Point Pleasant, along Highway 62. After a couple of turns in the road, you find yourself surrounded by wilderness. The landscape is overgrown with trees and dotted with bogs.

Ty pulls the car off the road and parks in what feels like the middle of nowhere.

"Hidden in these woods," Ty says, motioning around you, "are many of those bunkers I mentioned. Come, I'll show you."

He hops out of the car. You reach into the back seat and grab your backpack full of gear. Then you follow him as he leads you through clumps of trees and around swampy areas.

"See that mound up ahead?" Ty asks, pointing to a small rise covered in shrubs. "That's one of the bunkers."

You walk around it. On the opposite side is an entryway with its doors hanging from their hinges. A tunnel leads into the mound.

"Come on," Ty says, pulling out a flashlight.

You pull a flashlight out of your backpack and follow him. Inside, the bunker is a huge concrete dome. It is empty, with graffiti covering the walls.

"How many of these bunkers are there?" you ask.

"Don't know," Ty replies. "I've explored a few, but some have become so overgrown, nobody knows where they are anymore."

"Let's check out another one," you say to Ty.

Turn the page.

After stomping around the woods some more, you come across another bunker. Once inside, you notice this one isn't empty. There are bottles and food wrappers scattered about, and burnt sticks are piled up on one side.

"Looks like someone, or something, is living in here," Ty says.

"Think it could be the Mothman?" you ask.

Ty shrugs his shoulders.

You know someone—or something—has been in this bunker recently. It might be worth staking out to discover if this is the Mothman's lair. Then again, Ty did say there were more bunkers in the area. You could go check out another one to see if it looks even more promising.

To stake out the bunker, turn to page 22.
To explore another bunker, turn to page 25.

Common belief is that the Mothman first appeared to warn people about the Silver Bridge collapse. There are even those who claim to have seen the creature on the bridge shortly before the accident. If something bad is about to happen again, you want to be there to stop it. So you decide to go check out the new bridge.

On the way, Ty stops at the Mothman Museum in downtown Point Pleasant. Outside the museum stands a large, silver statue of the monster with its wings spread wide.

Point Pleasant's huge, metal statue of the Mothman was erected in 2003.

Turn the page.

"I hope it's not that scary in real life," you say.

The monster looks horrifying with its red eyes, and the creature towers over you.

"Probably even scarier, especially if you run across it at night," Ty adds with a smile.

Then you enter the museum. From the outside, the building looks like an ordinary shop. But once inside, you are amazed at everything you see. There are more statues—one even hangs from the ceiling. You read old newspaper clippings and police reports about sightings of the creature. There is also an exhibit about the Men in Black.

Rumor has it that the Men in Black are secret government agents who silence anyone who claims to have seen a UFO. You've never run across them while chasing after mythical creatures—and you hope to keep it that way.

"I thought the Men in Black only showed up at UFO sightings," you say to Ty.

"Some people believe the Mothman might be a creature from another world," Ty explains.

You also read about the collapse of the Silver Bridge. Forty-six people died, making it one of the deadliest bridge collapses in U.S. history.

The new Silver Memorial Bridge replaced the old bridge in 1969. It crosses the Ohio River into the small town of Gallipolis, Ohio.

"On which side of the river should we begin our investigation—the Ohio side or the West Virginia side?" Ty asks.

To cross to the Ohio side, turn to page 27.
To stay on the West Virginia side, turn to page 29.

There's no doubt that this bunker has been used recently. You think it could even be the Mothman's hangout. Stories about the creature began in this area, and some people claim it still dwells here.

Likely in one of these bunkers, you think. *Maybe even this one.*

You tell Ty you'd like to stake out this bunker to see if the Mothman appears. He agrees. The place is a bit of a mess, but you find a spot to sit. Then you turn off your flashlights and wait.

Spooky, abandoned bunkers often become linked to local legends.

Being a cryptozoologist involves a lot of waiting around, hoping to see something interesting. But you're lucky you don't have to wait long this time. Shortly after getting comfortable, you hear a noise.

No, not just a noise, you think. *Voices.*

Then there is a blinding flash of light shining on you.

"Hey, who are—," a voice begins. "Oh, Ty, why are hiding out in the dark?"

Suddenly, three people Ty knows surround you. They are all monster hunters like you.

"We thought the Mothman might be living in this bunker," you say.

One of Ty's friends picks up a food wrapper and says, "Only if it likes potato chips."

Turn the page.

What you learn is that Ty's friends have been using this bunker as a base for their search for the Mothman. That explains the food wrappers and pile of burnt sticks where they built a fire.

"But we've been out here for days," one of them says.

"And we haven't seen a thing," another says.

If experienced monster hunters haven't seen anything in the TNT Area, you know it's a waste to spend any more time here. You share stories with Ty's friends as you help them clean up the bunker. Then you and Ty head out.

While you didn't find proof that the Mothman exists, you at least made some new connections in the cryptozoologist world.

THE END

To read another adventure, turn to page 11.
To learn more about the Mothman, turn to page 101.

Looking around at the bottles and food wrappers, you think some kids—rather than a fearsome monster—have been hanging out here. So you and Ty decide to look for another bunker.

You hike deeper into the woods. Before long, you spot a small opening through some brush.

"Is there something through there?" you ask.

"I dunno," Ty says. "Let's check it out."

To your surprise, you find a door to another bunker. It's half buried, and the door is either stuck shut or locked—it's hard to tell with all the dirt and brush piled up against it.

"Do you think something could be hiding in there?" you ask Ty.

He shrugs and says, "Hard to say. I've never seen this bunker before."

Turn the page.

You're not sure what to do. This bunker is unlike the others. The first couple you saw were sturdy and seemed safe to enter. This bunker is sunken into the mucky ground and you wonder if it has collapsed inside—which could make it dangerous. Maybe it would be safer to explore a different bunker.

On the other hand, a locked door is hard to resist. You are really curious about what might be inside. A hidden bunker that no one knows about would be a great place for the Mothman to hide.

To explore a different bunker, turn to page 31.
To break open this bunker, turn to page 33.

"Let's swing over to the Ohio side of the river," you tell Ty.

That way you'll see the new bridge. Well, at more than 50 years old, it's not exactly "new." But if the Mothman is here because it might collapse, maybe it's hanging out on the bridge.

Ty drives while you sit in the passenger seat.

To you, the bridge looks like any other. It is a busy day, and traffic fills all four lanes of the highway. A divider runs down the middle to separate the oncoming traffic.

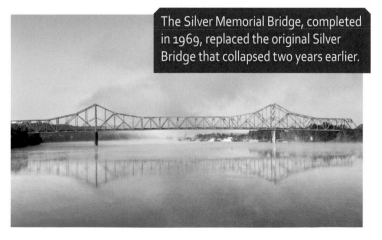

The Silver Memorial Bridge, completed in 1969, replaced the original Silver Bridge that collapsed two years earlier.

Turn the page.

"It's a cantilever bridge," Ty tells you. "Its metal, cage-like structure supports the roadway."

As you stare out the window, watching the metal beams buzz by, you suddenly notice a dark figure atop the metal frame. It's large, with wings.

Could that be the Mothman?, you wonder.

This could be your chance to get a photo of the creature. You could ask Ty stop so you can take a picture—but he'd have to do so in the middle of traffic. Or you could keep going to the other side of the bridge and circle back to get a photo. Problem is, whatever is up there might fly away by then.

To stop to take pictures, turn to page 34.
To keep going and circle back, turn to page 35.

The legend of the Mothman began in West Virginia, and—for that reason alone—you decide to stick to this side of the river.

You follow the Ohio River toward the Silver Memorial Bridge. Ty parks along the road just before the on-ramp to cross the bridge. You get a good view of the metal structure that forms the bridge.

"It's a cantilever bridge," Ty says, explaining that the bridge's frame holds up the roadway.

Then you spot something high up on the bridge. It's hard to make out from this far away, but there's a large, dark figure in the tangle of metal beams. You grab your camera and start taking video footage as it spreads its wings.

It's gotta be the Mothman, you think.

Then the creature takes flight and dips down below the bridge, toward the river.

Turn the page.

That could be it. The video you just took could be all the proof you need to convince people that the Mothman exists. You're excited to post your images online to see what others think. On the other hand, maybe the creature is hiding under the bridge. It'd be a long, treacherous hike through some rough-looking terrain to get to the base of the bridge. But maybe you'll find even more evidence of the Mothman if you investigate further.

To post your images, turn to page 41.
To investigate further, turn to page 43.

Monster hunting is risky business. You never know what might be lurking in the shadows. You tend to steer away from visible dangers, like creepy old bunkers that look like they might collapse on you. So instead of trying to break into this one, you decide it's best to continue your search for the Mothman elsewhere.

While it is starting to get late, you hope to at least check out one more bunker. On the way back to the car, you find one with its door cracked open just enough for you to crawl through. You grab a flashlight and head inside.

Turn the page.

In one part of the bunker, you see a pile of leaves and brush that looks like it could be a bed or nest. In another part, you see dried-up animal bones.

"Something's been living in here," Ty says.

Just then, you hear a noise. *SREEECH!* It sounds like scraping at the door. You whirl your flashlights around and see a dark shape scrambling away.

"Was that the Mothman?" you ask Ty.

"Yeah, I think it could have been," he says.

You could chase after whatever it was, hoping to get some photos or other evidence that proves it is the Mothman. Or you could wait inside this bunker and hope that it returns. You might have a better chance of getting some photos of it then.

To run after whatever you saw, turn to page 37.
To wait inside the bunker, turn to page 39.

"The Mothman could be in here," you say to Ty. "This bunker is pretty hidden."

"Let's try to break into it," Ty says.

You both set to work trying to pry the door open. It takes some digging, some slamming of your shoulder against the door, and a little cursing. But eventually you get the door to creak open just a crack. Just enough for you to wiggle through on your belly.

Once inside, you reach back and start to say, "Ty, hand me my flash—"

But suddenly, there is a loud CRACK above you. Then huge chunks of concrete crash down as the bunker's roof caves in. Your world goes black, and your monster-hunting days are over.

THE END

To read another adventure, turn to page 11.
To learn more about the Mothman, turn to page 101.

You don't want to miss out on the rare chance to get a photo of a mythical creature.

"Stop!" you shout to Ty.

Ty is so startled that he slams on the brakes. The car skids to a stop in the middle of the road.

But before you can grab your camera, you hear a booming *HOOONK!* and a *SCREECH!* of brakes. That is followed by the *CRUNCH* of metal on metal as a semitruck rams into you.

Ty's car spins and rolls. When it stops, you're hanging upside down. You feel like throwing up, and you can't move your right arm. Then the pain hits you and your eyesight gets blurry.

Before you pass out, you hear someone say, "They're lucky they were wearing their seat belts."

THE END
To read another adventure, turn to page 11.
To learn more about the Mothman, turn to page 101.

You are surrounded by traffic. Stopping in the middle of the highway could be dangerous with all the cars and trucks whizzing by. You don't want to cause an accident. So it's best if you circle back.

"Hey, Ty, I think I saw something up on top of the bridge," you say.

"No way! Really?" he replies. "Could you tell if it was the Mothman?"

"No," you say. "But it was big and dark and had wings."

Once you reach the other side of the bridge, Ty hurries to turn around and cross back over. The whole time, you keep an eye out for the creature you saw. You scan the beams above for any sign of the dark, shadowy figure.

As you reach the middle of the bridge, you see it again—high above.

Turn the page.

"There!" you shout.

Ty slows down as you try to take some photos. It's hard to get a good shot. The car is moving, traffic is whizzing by, and the tangle of beams blocks your view of the creature at times.

Then you see it take flight. It swoops down and disappears below the bridge.

"Did you get some photos?" Ty asks.

"Yeah, I think I got some good ones," you say.

These images could be just what you need to prove that the Mothman exists. You could post them online, and then move on to hunt other monsters. Then again, it's possible the creature landed under the bridge. You could continue your investigation in hopes of finding even more evidence the Mothman exists.

To post your images online, turn to page 41.
To investigate further, turn to page 43.

This is your chance! The opportunity you have been waiting for. A legendary cryptid has just crossed your path, and you don't want to miss out on getting the evidence you need to prove the Mothman is real.

"Let's go after it!" you shout to Ty.

Then both of you scramble through the bunker's opening.

Ahead of you, you see a shadow darting between the trees. You give chase, ducking under branches and stomping through bogs.

Shadowy figures darting through a dark forest can be difficult to identify.

Turn the page.

At some point, Ty falls behind you.

As you are running, your leg catches on something. Then you are falling into darkness. You land hard as something hits the back of your head. Everything goes black.

Turns out you fell through the roof of one of the many forgotten bunkers in the TNT Area. When Ty can't find you, he calls 911. Emergency workers comb the area looking for you, but your body is never found. People begin to believe you fell victim to the Mothman.

THE END

To read another adventure, turn to page 11.
To learn more about the Mothman, turn to page 101.

Chasing shadows through an unfamiliar wilderness will only get you lost—or worse. If this is the Mothman's lair, it would be best to hunker down and see if it returns.

You and Ty find a comfortable spot inside the bunker to sit. Then you wait. And wait. And wait.

At one point in the night, you hear the scraping noise again. Then you see a pair of red eyes, low to the ground, peeking through the opening in the doorway.

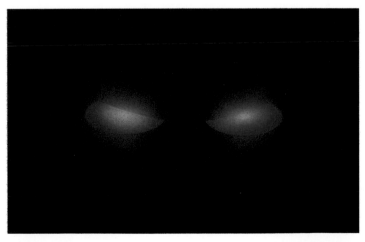

Turn the page.

You snap a few quick pictures with your smartphone. But as soon as you move, whatever it is runs away again.

You look at the photos you got. They are dark and blurry, and mostly just show the pair of red eyes. But they are at least something.

You don't know if what you saw was the Mothman, but you post online about your adventures in the TNT Area. You include the photos and ask people what they think. Many are skeptical, thinking it was just an animal, such as an opossum. Others are excited. They think you might have captured images of the Mothman.

It is hard to know for sure, but you count your trip a success as you've added to the legend of the mysterious Mothman.

THE END

To read another adventure, turn to page 11.
To learn more about the Mothman, turn to page 101.

You decide to post the images you captured of the Mothman. What you have is a little blurry and the figure is difficult to see in the distance. So you don't expect a lot of responses. The evidence you found isn't really that much better than anything you've dug up online. But it's at least something. It's more than you got while looking for Bigfoot.

You are surprised at the responses you get, though.

The Mothman is back! a reader comments.

Turn the page.

The bridge is going to collapse, another writes.

Yet another says, *This signals disaster!*

You receive hundreds of similar comments as many people believe that Mothman's presence on the bridge is a bad omen. They think another disaster is about to happen.

Word spreads. Unexpectedly, your posts start a panic. For weeks, people refuse to cross the bridge. The rumors cause traffic backups and all sorts of problems for residents of the area.

Then, when the bridge hasn't collapsed a month later, people claim you were just "crying wolf" and trying to get attention. While neither is true, the responses have damaged your reputation as a monster hunter.

THE END

To read another adventure, turn to page 11.
To learn more about the Mothman, turn to page 101.

The terrain between you and the base of the bridge is covered in shrubs and looks boggy. Soon you are trekking through muck and getting your arms scratched up by thick brush.

When you finally reach the base of the bridge, you are close to the river. You look down at the rocky shore and notice a large, grayish bird with long, skinny legs wading in the water.

"Aw, man," you groan. "I think what I saw up on the bridge was a heron!"

"Bummer," Ty replies. "I guess those photos you took are pretty useless."

You're disappointed you didn't get evidence of the Mothman. But at least you found the truth behind the creature on top of the bridge.

THE END

To read another adventure, turn to page 11.
To learn more about the Mothman, turn to page 101.

The steel and concrete jungle of Chicago, Illinois, has been rumored to hide the elusive Mothman.

CHAPTER 3

CHICAGO, ILLINOIS

While your friend Jackie is not as experienced as you at sitting up in trees and waiting for monsters to walk by, she knows what she's talking about when it comes to cryptids. She has one of the most popular blogs about strange monsters. So you're excited for the opportunity to meet up with her.

On your way to the Windy City, you two exchange several texts.

Sightings of the Chicago Mothman began about ten years ago, Jackie writes.

Is it the same creature as the Point Pleasant, West Virginia, Mothman? you ask.

Yes, I believe so, she replies.

Turn the page.

Then Jackie goes on to explain that the descriptions of the Mothman from both parts of the country are similar. It is said to be a dark, winged creature with glowing red eyes.

The only difference is where they were seen, she adds. *And, well, the Chicago sightings happened almost 50 years after the first Point Pleasant one.*

You also wonder about the common belief that the Mothman is a bad omen. In Point Pleasant, a bridge collapsed a year after it appeared and more than 40 people died. Many people believe the Mothman foretold the tragedy.

Did something bad happen after the Mothman was first seen in Chicago? you ask Jackie.

Nothing like the Silver Bridge collapse, she replies. *But there was a bad flood in 2017. That's the year most of the sightings were reported. But it's hard to say if there's really a connection.*

On your way to Chicago, you exchange a few more texts. You learn that many of the recent Mothman sightings occurred around Oz Park. It's in the Lincoln Park area of the city and not too far from Lake Michigan. You two agree to meet there—but the question is when.

You could go during the daytime to scope things out. An unfamiliar city can be just as dangerous as an unfamiliar wilderness. Maybe you could also find a good place to stake out and wait for the monster.

Or you could meet up with her at night. You likely won't have time to set up any of your surveillance gear. But night is when most monster hunting occurs.

To check out the park during the day, turn to page 48.
To check out the park at night, turn to page 50.

Let's meet up at noon, you text Jackie.

You figure it's best to explore the area while it's still light out. Jackie can show you around, and then you can find a good place to stake out later that night. If you find a good open area, you could even set up some motion-sensing cameras.

You meet Jackie at Oz Park, which takes up several city blocks. You start by just walking around, to get a feel for the area. The park has a tennis court in the southeast corner, and the northeast corner has a few trees. On the west side is a large field for baseball and softball. You also see people strolling throughout the park enjoying the day.

"You're the experienced monster hunter," Jackie says. "Where do we start?"

"Well, it's a fairly big park, so we need to decide what area to stake out," you say.

Oz Park features several statues of characters from Frank Baum's classic book *The Wonderful Wizard of Oz*. Baum once lived in the neighborhood near the park.

Then you go on to explain that the trees on the east side of the park might provide a great hiding place for the Mothman. Then again, the field on the west side has a lot of open space. That would allow you to get some great footage if you set up some motion-sensing cameras.

To stake out the east side of the park, turn to page 51.
To stake out the west side of the park, turn to page 54.

You're used to monster hunting at night, and you want to get right down to business. You tell Jackie to meet you just before sunset.

There's a tennis court on the south side of the park, she texts. *Let's meet there.*

OK, you reply.

True to her word, you find Jackie near the tennis court, right around sunset.

"So where do we start?" she asks.

"Let's explore the park," you say.

It is a sizable park, taking up a few city blocks. A monster could be hiding anywhere. You could start by taking one of the many paths through the park. Or you could walk around the outskirts of the park.

To walk through the park, turn to page 57.
To walk around the park, turn to page 59.

The east side of the park has more trees. While it may not be a great place to set up your cameras—because of the trees—it seems like the perfect place for a monster to hide. But first, there is one important thing you must do.

"Have you ever been on a monster stakeout?" you ask Jackie.

She shakes her head no.

"Well, then, the first thing we need to do is get snacks," you say with a smile.

"Right on," Jackie replies.

You and Jackie go get all the supplies you need. Along with snacks, you load your backpack with flashlights, a first-aid kit, and some camera equipment. But mostly, you plan on using your smartphone to take photos and video. You also dress all in black, from your black hiking boots to your black stocking cap.

Turn the page.

Although Oz Park isn't huge and doesn't have a lot of trees, there many places for big and small creatures to hide.

Once you're all set, you and Jackie find a quiet spot on the east side of the park to sit and wait.

And you wait. And wait. And wait.

"We do this a lot," you whisper to Jackie. "Sit and wait."

She smiles and nods.

At some point in the night, you hear a *whoosh* of wings overhead.

"What was that?" Jackie whispers, but all you can do is shrug. You have no idea.

Then you hear a loud screech coming from a nearby tree.

"Does the Mothman make noises like that?" you whisper.

This time, it's Jackie's turn to shrug.

"The reports I've read never mention it making any noise," she says.

Something is in the trees nearby. You're guessing it doesn't know you're there, hiding in the shadows. You could continue to wait, hoping it might come closer, so you can see what it is. Or you could head in the direction of the noise. Of course, whatever it is might notice you and take off. But you also might have a better chance of seeing it.

To wait, turn to page 61.
To follow the sound, turn to page 63.

"The west side of the park has a lot of open space," you say. "We could set up some cameras and let them do all the work for us."

"Sounds like a plan," Jackie says.

It takes you a while to get your cameras in place. But by the time you finish, you have every corner of the field covered.

Now all you need to do is wait for nightfall. Jackie parked her car nearby, so you hunker down inside. You pull out a laptop and link it to your cameras. They have a night vision mode, so as it gets dark, you can still see what's happening in the park.

And then you wait. And wait. And wait.

Throughout the night you and Jackie take turns watching the monitor while the other naps.

At one point, you are awoken by a gasp.

"Look!" Jackie shouts.

You quickly glance over at the computer screen. You see a large, dark figure flying across the park.

"Let's go!" you shout to Jackie. Then you both leap from the car. You hope to spot the creature before it flies off.

When the two of you reach the field, you spot a large, dark shadow disappearing behind some distant trees. It is flying to the east, toward the shore of Lake Michigan.

"Let's keep following it," you tell Jackie, "Maybe it'll land somewhere we can get some photos of it."

As you are crossing the park, you hear a sudden ruckus coming from the northeast corner of the park. People are shouting excitedly.

Turn the page.

"Should we see what's going on?" Jackie asks.

You don't know. Whatever you saw was flying toward the lake. You could keep going in that direction in hopes of catching another glimpse of it. Or you could go see what all the noise is about to the northeast. Someone could be in danger, or maybe people there also saw the creature.

To go toward the lake, turn to page 66.
To go toward the noise, turn to page 69.

The sidewalks around the park are lit up with streetlights. You figure a monster would definitely steer clear of them. But a large area inside the park is wooded, which would be a perfect place for a mythical beast to hide.

You head into the park, down one of its many paths. You look up in trees for any sign of the Mothman. You explore any shadowy space for what might be hidden in it.

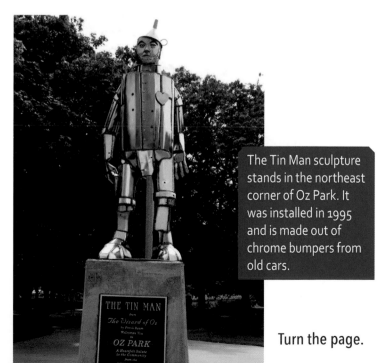

The Tin Man sculpture stands in the northeast corner of Oz Park. It was installed in 1995 and is made out of chrome bumpers from old cars.

Turn the page.

Monster hunting in the city is a lot different than out in the woods. There are fewer hidden dangers, like venomous snakes or tree roots to trip you up. So you are less afraid of exploring the dark areas of the park.

As it grows darker, the park becomes quieter and more still. There are fewer people about and less noise to distract you.

That's when you see a dark shadow dart between some trees. It's too quick for you to snap a photo with your smartphone.

"What was that?" Jackie gasps.

Then you see the dark shadow rise above the trees and fly off to the east. It's heading toward the shore of Lake Michigan.

"I have no idea," you shout. "But come on, let's follow it."

Turn to page 66.

It's getting darker. While a city park at night might be the perfect place for the monster to hide, you want to get a feel for the area around the park first. It's never a good idea to stumble about in the dark.

You walk around the tennis court and reach a corner of the park. You turn north, to walk along its eastern side. The farther you go, the more trees you see.

Then you hear a loud ruckus up ahead. It's coming from the north end of the park. People are shouting excitedly. From where you stand, you can't be sure what is going on. Is something wrong? Did someone get hurt?

"Should we go check it out?" Jackie asks.

You're not sure what to do. All that noise might scare away the very monster you are hunting tonight.

Turn the page.

You could leave the park and walk around the block to keep searching the area instead. Or you could continue on toward the noise. Maybe you could help with whatever is happening—or maybe people are shouting because they saw the Mothman.

To leave the park, turn to page 64.
To go toward the noise, turn to page 69.

You're pretty sure whatever is out there hasn't seen you yet, and you don't want to scare it away. So you keep still and wait.

A moment later, Jackie shouts, "Look!"

A pair of reddish eyes stare at you from a leafy tree branch. You quickly snap some photos.

Then something spooks whatever is in the tree. It spreads its wings and takes flight. In the dark, all you see is a large, shadowy figure rising in the air and disappearing into the night.

A face-to-face encounter with the Mothman in the moonlight would be an exhilarating—if not terrifying—experience.

Turn the page.

You take more photos.

"Was that the Mothman?" Jackie asks.

You shrug. You really aren't sure. It kind of fits the description, with the wings and red eyes. But the photos you took don't clearly show what it was. The creature just appears as a large shadow perched in the trees.

You and Jackie post your pictures online and tell the story of your adventures that night. A few people respond by saying they also saw the same creature near the park. But no one has any better photos than you. While you do not have definitive proof that the Mothman exists, you at least have a great story to tell. If nothing else, it helps increase your and Jackie's reputations as monster hunters.

THE END

To read another adventure, turn to page 11.
To learn more about the Mothman, turn to page 101.

This is your chance. The Mothman might be on the other side of some trees, so you and Jackie chase after it.

Soon, you hear another screech and then a rustle in the trees as something launches into the sky. All you can see is a large shadow before the creature disappears behind some more trees.

"What was it?" Jackie asks. "Was that the Mothman?"

You don't know. All you saw was a large, winged shadow flying off. But worse, you scared it away before you could snap any pictures.

Your hunt for the Mothman ends in failure. All you have is a story to tell without any proof that you saw the cryptid. No one will believe you.

THE END

To read another adventure, turn to page 11.
To learn more about the Mothman, turn to page 101.

You don't want to get involved with whatever is going on up ahead. The noise is likely ruining your chances of spotting the Mothman. So you turn down a side street.

The Mothman has been seen "around" the park. That also includes the surrounding neighborhood.

You turn down another street to get farther away from the noise the people were making. You're not very familiar with the area. Neither is Jackie. She just knows that this is where recent Mothman sightings have occurred.

Suddenly, two shadowy figures step out of the night and surround you. Only they don't have wings or red, glowing eyes like the Mothman. They are just a couple of people.

"What's in your backpack?" one of them asks.

"Hand it over," the other one says, grabbing your pack away from you.

In the end, the pair takes your backpack filled with expensive camera gear.

It's disappointing that you didn't come across the Mothman. And to top it off, you had some of your gear stolen. This monster hunt has been a complete bust for you.

THE END

To read another adventure, turn to page 11.
To learn more about the Mothman, turn to page 101.

You head in the direction the shadowy figure flew. Jackie races after you. You leave the park and start running down the city streets. Every now and then you think you see the creature darting between buildings. But it is always just too far ahead of you to get a good look at it. And you don't dare stop to take a picture.

Then, after several blocks, a park spreads out in front of you near the shore of Lake Michigan.

"The Lincoln Park Zoo is up ahead," Jackie tells you.

Through some trees you can even see the entrance to the zoo. As you head toward it, you see a man in a zookeeper uniform. He is walking around and looking up in the trees.

"Hey, you," he calls over. "You didn't happen to see an owl flying about, did you?"

You walk over and tell him that you saw something with a big wingspan.

"Snowy owls are one of the largest species. Ours recently escaped and has a wingspan of about five feet," the zookeeper says.

"What color are its eyes?" Jackie asks.

"Mostly yellow," the zookeeper says. "But at night, they can glow orange, or even reddish."

The Lincoln Park Zoo was founded in 1868, making it one of the oldest zoos in the United States.

Turn the page.

You and Jackie look at each other. You know by the way her shoulders slump that she is thinking the same thing as you. The recent sightings of the Mothman were likely just an escaped owl.

The discovery is disappointing. But you know that this is all part of monster hunting. More often than not, the leads you follow are false ones. This trip turns out to be a bust. But at least you got to hang out with Jackie and learn more about the Mothman from her.

THE END

To read another adventure, turn to page 11.
To learn more about the Mothman, turn to page 101.

"Let's see what's going on," you tell Jackie.

Maybe the excited shouts are because someone saw the very creature you are after. Maybe not. You don't know, and you won't unless you check it out.

When you reach the north end of the park, you see a small crowd of people pointing and staring up at a nearby building.

"What's all the excitement about?" you ask a man.

"There was someone up there," he says, motioning to the building.

"Not someone," a women cuts in. "*Something!* It had red, glowing eyes."

"Whatever it was, it flew up there," another person adds.

Turn the page.

As you are talking to the crowd, a police car pulls up. An officer gets out of the passenger side and walks over.

"What's going on here?" she asks.

Do you reply to her? Do you tell her that the people gathered here have seen the Mothman? Maybe then you'd have the help of law enforcement officials in your hunt for the cryptid. Or do you stay quiet? If you do, you could interview the people you've been talking to and post their stories online.

To tell the officer what you saw, go to page 71.

To interview the people, turn to page 73.

Searching for a monster in a big city like Chicago feels like an impossible task. Sure, you have Jackie's help. But what if you had the help of law enforcement officers? Their assistance with your hunt would surely be a success.

"We've seen the Mothman," you tell the officer, pointing up to the building. "Up there, and we could use your help tracking it down."

"The what?" she asks, shaking her head.

"The Mothman. You know, it's got red, glowing eyes and huge wings," Jackie says.

The officer looks dumbfounded. "Is this some sort of joke?" she asks.

But before you can explain further, another police car pulls up next to the first one. Several officers get out of the cars to disperse the crowd.

Turn the page.

As that is happening, the first officer walks over to you.

"I have better things to do than follow up with some prank," she says. Then she tells you and Jackie to leave the area and go home.

Your monster hunt is over for the night. Worse, you lose your partner. After the incident with the police, Jackie decides she would rather stick to doing research and working on her blog. Without her help, you decide that this monster-hunting trip is a failure.

THE END

To read another adventure, turn to page 11.
To learn more about the Mothman, turn to page 101.

The Mothman is a mythical creature. You doubt the police officer will believe it was just up on a building in Chicago. Instead of telling her about the Mothman, you ask the people you were talking to if you can interview them.

While the officer breaks up the crowd, you, Jackie, and a couple of folks head over to a local coffee shop. You ask them questions about what they saw and record them on video.

While you don't get proof that the Mothman exists, your interviews are a hit. When you and Jackie post them online, they are viewed thousands of times. Even though you and Jackie didn't track down the Mothman, you both increase your reputations as monster hunters.

THE END

To read another adventure, turn to page 11.
To learn more about the Mothman, turn to page 101.

The La Crescenta-Montrose-Glendale communities are located in Los Angeles County in southern California. The area is nestled along the southern base of the San Gabriel Mountains.

CHAPTER 4

LA CRESCENTA, CALIFORNIA

You decide to head to Los Angeles. Gino is incredibly well known in the monster-hunting world. You might say he's even a bit of a celebrity. No other cryptozoologist is more popular than him with his many thousands of followers. The videos he's created of his adventures have millions of views. You are excited for and honored by the opportunity to join him in his search for the Mothman.

When he meets you, he's already filming.

"Wave for the camera!" he tells you.

"Hey," you say, waving shyly.

Turn the page.

"I'm going to record our entire expedition, if you don't mind," he says.

"As long as you're not live-streaming," you say.

Some embarrassing things can happen while on a monster hunt, like shrieking when something startles you in the middle of the night during a stakeout. You don't want awkward moments posted online. They could ruin your reputation.

"No, don't worry. I'm sure there will be some things—like bathroom breaks and boring moments where all we do is wait—that we'll edit out," Gino says with a smile.

Then you two sit down to chat about your expedition. Gino tells you that there have been a few Mothman sightings in neighboring La Crescenta. Most occurred north of town in a wilderness area with hiking trails.

"They sound like your typical Mothman sightings," he says. "A large, shadowy creature was seen up in the trees at night. Some reports say it had wings and red eyes."

But there have also been a few interesting sightings in town that Gino tells you about.

"Kids claim to have seen the Mothman walking down the streets of La Crescenta in broad daylight," Gino says, sounding astonished.

Then he asks which location you would like to investigate.

To investigate in the wilderness area, turn to page 78.

To investigate in town, turn to page 81.

You are not so sure about the sighting that occurred in broad daylight. That does not sound like your typical Mothman sighting. But reports about some strange creature being seen in the middle of a wilderness area at night? That's more like it.

North of the La Crescenta area is the Angeles National Forest. It is a mountainous region covered in trees. There are also lots of hiking trails. It was along some of these trails that people claim to have seen the Mothman.

"We should get an early start tomorrow," Gino says. "We'll have a lot of ground to cover."

The next morning, you meet him at a trailhead. You both have backpacks full of survival gear, including first-aids kits, fresh water, and snacks for the day.

Angeles National Forest has rugged terrain that can challenge even the most experienced hikers.

Then you begin your hike. It is a slow, steady climb up the mountains. The trail you are on starts off in a woodsy area. But higher up, you notice that the tree cover dwindles.

During the day, you are mostly sightseeing. You take photos and enjoy the fresh air. But as sunset nears, you pay more attention to the noises around you and any shadowy shapes you see within the forest. All the while, Gino films you and records commentary about you being a monster hunter in action.

Turn the page.

In fact, Gino is so busy recording you that he doesn't notice a large, dark shadow in the tree behind him. But you do.

"Behind you!" you shout.

Gino whips his phone around to capture video of something darting through the trees.

"I think I got it!" he shouts as the creature disappears into the night.

Most often, you don't even get a glimpse of the creature you are hunting. But Gino got some video of it. You could be satisfied with that. It is getting dark, after all, and you don't know how long you want to be in the mountains at night. Or, you could try to follow the creature. You would have to head off-trail, but maybe you'll get a clearer shot of what was up in the trees.

To stick with the video you captured, turn to page 83.
To chase after the creature, turn to page 85.

"Let's check out the sighting in town," you say. "It sounds pretty unusual."

Gino agrees. Most sightings of the Mothman occur at night, not in broad daylight. So there is something different going on here. You're interested in checking it out.

You make plans to meet up tomorrow at a park near the center of town.

* * *

The next day, you find Gino sitting on a swing with a big bag at his feet. It's full of surveillance gear, like motion-sensing cameras and microphones.

"You ready to get started?" he asks as he pulls out his smartphone to start recording you.

"Sure thing," you say.

Turn the page.

"How do you want to do this stakeout?" he asks. "There is plenty of tree cover around the park if we want to just hide out and wait." Then he taps the bag at his feet. "Or we could set up some surveillance gear to help us keep an eye on things."

Setting up the motion-sensing cameras takes a lot of time and work. You're not sure it is worth the effort if reports say the Mothman has been seen here in broad daylight. Hopefully the creature will be easy to spot. Then again, cameras are great monster-hunting tools. They catch things that you might miss if you look away or doze off—which has happened to you before on stakeouts.

To find a spot to hide out, turn to page 86.
To set up the cameras, turn to page 88.

You and Gino are excited to have gotten some video. It shows a large, dark creature lurking in the trees, but neither of you can be certain what it is. Still, you want Gino to post it online to get some other people's opinions and see if anyone thinks what you saw might be the Mothman.

However, when Gino posts the video he doesn't admit that you don't know what it shows. He says that you two definitely saw the Mothman and have the video footage to prove it.

But many of his thousands of followers do not buy it. The figure is difficult to see. It's hidden in the shadows of a tree, and it only appears for a brief moment before it disappears. Also, it shows none of the telltale signs of the Mothman. No red, glowing eyes. No wings. Gino's followers start posting comments about how you two are frauds.

Turn the page.

In the end, you are disappointed with your adventure with Gino. You thought his popularity would help boost your reputation as a monster hunter. But he fell short by claiming you had proof of the Mothman's existence with an inconclusive video at best. You just hope the experience doesn't harm your credibility as a cryptozoologist.

THE END

To read another adventure, turn to page 11.
To learn more about the Mothman, turn to page 101.

Sure, it's dark out, and you are in an unfamiliar area. But this is what monster hunting is all about. Taking risks!

You head in the direction that the shadowy creature disappeared. Gino is right behind you. But instead of scanning the trees for whatever it is you saw, he is taking video of you.

At one point, you hear a rustle in a tree. As you go to investigate, you hear a grumbling noise. Then you see the shadowy creature again, just ahead of you. It darts between two boulders.

It seems like whatever you are following is just ahead of you. Do you keep chasing after it, hoping to see what it is? Or do you turn back? It is getting darker, and you are scrambling through dangerous mountainous terrain.

To continue on, turn to page 90.
To turn back, turn to page 92.

"Let's not waste time setting up all your gear," you say. "With two of us, we should be able to spot whatever comes lurking around the park."

Gino switches his smartphone so he's recording himself in selfie mode.

"You hear that, all you monster hunters out there?" he says. "We're doing this old school—so bust out the snacks!"

The two of you find a spot in the park where you can hide behind some trees and still see all the paths leading into and around the park. Then you hunker down and wait. Along with the surveillance gear, Gino made sure to pack all the essentials for a stakeout, including your favorite snacks.

At some point in the day, Gino elbows you.

"Hey, what's that?" he says, pointing to a dark shape between some trees.

The figure is tall enough to be the Mothman. But you don't see any wings, and it's too far away to clearly see what it is. Then, suddenly, it disappears behind some trees.

"Whoa, that's exactly what the kids say they saw," Gino says. "A dark figure that mysteriously disappeared."

Gino was recording everything, so you have footage of the strange figure. You could post it online, stating you might have just seen the Mothman. Gino earned a lot of his popularity through posting videos of stuff like this. Or you could go investigate further. Maybe there is more evidence to find.

To post the footage, turn to page 94.
To follow the shadowy figure, turn to page 95.

During monster hunts, motion-sensing cameras have always been your greatest tool. Their night mode can see things in the dark that you can't. And they are always watching, so you won't miss a thing if you look away for a moment.

The only downside is it takes a lot of time to set them up. You have to find spots with clear views. You also need to make sure they are recording correctly and that you get them linked to your computer so you can monitor them.

At some point while you're working, you swear you see a dark shadow out of the corner of your eye. You turn, but there's nothing there.

Using motion-sensing cameras in the wilderness is a great way to take photos of any creatures that pass near them.

You don't think much about it, but later that day—after hours of staring at your computer and seeing nothing—you wonder about the dark shadow you saw.

Could that have been the Mothman? you think. *Could I have been too busy setting up the cameras to have seen its approach? Did Gino and I unknowingly scare it off?*

You ask yourself many questions as you sit and wait. By the end of the day, there is no sign of the Mothman. And even though you stake out the park for the next two days, you have a similar lack of success.

You hate to admit it, but your hunt for the Mothman ends in failure.

THE END

To read another adventure, turn to page 11.
To learn more about the Mothman, turn to page 101.

With the creature just ahead of you, you don't want to give up now. It really seems like you are on the verge of catching it.

As you crawl over some rocks, chasing the creature, you hear a noise that startles you.

"Ahhh!" Gino screams.

You turn, but there is no sign of him.

"Gino?" you whisper, afraid the creature you were chasing got him.

"Down here," Gino groans.

While you were racing headlong through the wilderness, Gino had continued to film you. He was paying more attention to where you were going than to what was in front of him. While you had skirted around a small cliff just moments ago, he stepped right off it.

Luckily, he didn't fall far, but he landed hard. When you look down, you can see he's limping on one leg.

"Think I sprained my ankle," he says.

There is something else you see that gets your attention. At Gino's feet is the smartphone he'd been using to record your adventures—and it's smashed.

Not only is Gino hurt, but you've lost all proof that you were out here chasing the Mothman. It's a long walk back to town as you help your injured friend down the mountain. All the while, you're left thinking about your missed opportunity to capture proof of the Mothman that might be haunting these woods.

THE END

To read another adventure, turn to page 11.
To learn more about the Mothman, turn to page 101.

Angeles National Forest's dry, rocky landscape can be dangerous to traverse whether it is day or night.

To be a monster hunter, you have to be fearless. But that is much different than being foolish. It is getting dark. You are racing over rocky terrain and darting between trees while trying to chase down some shadowy figure. It's only going to get more dangerous the darker it gets, and a part of you is a little afraid of catching up to a monster in the middle of the night.

"Let's turn back," you tell Gino. "We're never going to catch whatever it is, and it's getting late. We have a long hike back down the mountain."

"No worries," Gino says. "I got some great video of you in action."

The next day, he shows you the video. It is pretty amazing. There are glimpses of something up in the trees. Gino also has video of you scrambling over rocks and scanning trees when you heard the grumbling noise.

After doing some editing, he posts the video online. Sure, it doesn't show the Mothman or prove that the cryptid exists. But people are excited to see you in action. They think you are fearless as you chase after the shadowy creature. You may not have proven the existence of the Mothman, but you do increase your credibility among cryptozoologists.

THE END

To read another adventure, turn to page 11.
To learn more about the Mothman, turn to page 101.

"We got what we need," Gino says, excitedly. "This is our proof. Proof that the Mothman is real. What do you think?"

You aren't so sure, but you let him post the video online. People will be excited to see what you've seen—at least that's what you hope.

But the feedback isn't positive.

That's no proof, one commenter types.

No wings? No red, glowing eyes? No Mothman! another types.

"This is going to ruin my rep!" Gino exclaims. Then he takes the video down. Even worse, he calls off the whole monster hunt. He doesn't want to risk any more negative feedback. Without his help, you must admit failure and go home.

THE END

To read another adventure, turn to page 11.
To learn more about the Mothman, turn to page 101.

Sure, Gino shot some video of the dark figure, but is it enough proof to say you saw the Mothman? You don't think so. You want more evidence before you post anything online.

"Come on, let's follow it," you say to Gino.

While you take off running, he lags behind. He is capturing video of you as you give chase.

In the distance, the shadowy figure darts around a building. You race down the block and stop where you saw it turn. You see some people talking in front of a coffee shop, but you don't see anything that resembles the Mothman.

Then Gino catches up to you. He is holding his smartphone up. Since you don't see the Mothman, you wonder if you should tell him to keep recording or ask him to stop.

To keep recording, turn to page 96.
To stop recording, turn to page 99.

"Keep recording, Gino. I swear I saw the Mothman," you say. "It just darted around this corner."

You want him to keep recording just in case it pops back into view down the street.

But then the unexpected happens. A man standing in front of the coffee shop looks over at you. He whispers to his friends, and then he starts stomping in your direction.

"Hey, you!" the man shouts. "Are you following me?"

He is wearing dark clothes and a long, black overcoat. You can tell from the sound of his voice that he is angry.

"Did those kids put you up to this?" the man shouts. "I told them I am not the Mothman, so stop following me."

That is all you needed to hear.

You turn to Gino and say, "Let's get out of here!"

What you thought was a lead to uncovering the Mothman's existence turned out to be a hoax. The kids Gino had talked to must not have seen anything but a man in dark clothes. You aren't sure if they knew it was just a man, or if they thought the man was the Mothman. You have read about cases where an ordinary person was mistaken for the Mothman.

You are disappointed that you didn't actually come across the creepy cryptid. But that is not the worst part of your adventure. Gino was recording you the whole time. And the next day, he posts video of you running down the street and then being confronted by the angry man.

Turn the page.

At first you are simply angry at Gino. But then you start reading all the comments from Gino's thousands of followers.

What a fraud, one posts.

That guy should sue you for harassment, another posts.

Your embarrassment grows as the comments continue to pour in. You are not sure your reputation as a monster hunter will survive the negative feedback.

THE END

To read another adventure, turn to page 11.
To learn more about the Mothman, turn to page 101.

There is nothing to see. The Mothman is gone, so you ask Gino to stop recording.

"Maybe we have enough footage to at least post," he says.

As you turn to walk away, you notice the people in front of the coffee shop looking at you and whispering to each other. You wonder if they've seen Gino's videos. He is pretty popular in the area for his monster-hunting exploits.

That night, Gino post the videos. You are excited to see the number of views shoot up as people start watching. The dark figure you captured on film isn't definitive proof that the Mothman exists, but it sparks people's imagination. In the end, it also helps improve your reputation as a cryptozoologist.

THE END

To read another adventure, turn to page 11.
To learn more about the Mothman, turn to page 101.

With glowing red eyes and ragged wings, the Mothman looks like a creature born in the realm of nightmares.

CHAPTER 5

HISTORY OF THE MOTHMAN

The legend of the Mothman began in the fall of 1966. While working one night, a group of gravediggers saw something strange in the trees surrounding the Clendenin cemetery not far from Point Pleasant, West Virginia. They claimed a large, winged, humanlike creature flew overhead.

A few nights later, on November 15, Roger and Linda Scarberry were out with Steve and Mary Mallette. They were driving along State Highway 62 near the old ammunition factory, a few miles north of Point Pleasant. Suddenly, a strange figure appeared in the car's headlights.

The couples guessed the figure stood 7 feet (2.1 meters) tall. They said it looked like a muscular man with white, angel-like wings and large eyes that glowed red. They also claimed the creature chased them as they raced back to town at up to 100 miles (161 kilometers) per hour.

When the couples reported what they saw to local law enforcement, their claims were dismissed. The county sheriff said it was likely a type of heron. These tall, water-wading birds can stand a couple of feet tall and have wingspans several feet wide. Some even have reddish eyes.

The two couples also reported what they saw to the local newspaper. Their story was printed in the *Point Pleasant Register* with the headline "Couples See Man-Sized Bird . . . Creature . . . Something."

The newspaper article sparked a rash of sightings. People throughout the area claimed

Some people believe the appearance of the Mothman in 1966 was a bad omen that foretold the 1967 collapse of the Silver Bridge.

to have seen a mysterious creature—soon to be called the Mothman—along the Ohio River. There were also reports about the Mothman killing people's pets.

The creature likely would have remained a local legend if not for journalist John Keel. Keel started off researching UFOs and aliens. But in 1975, he published *The Mothman Prophecies: A True Story*. The book detailed his investigation into the Mothman and helped popularize the idea that the creature came to forewarn people of the Silver Bridge collapse a year later.

Since Keel's book, the Mothman legend has grown. Sightings have been reported across the United States, in places like Chicago and the Los Angeles area, as well as around the world.

People have also linked the Mothman to several notable disasters. These include the nuclear meltdown at Chernobyl, Ukraine, in 1986, and the collapse of the World Trade Center towers in New York in 2001.

There is a lot of speculation about how the Mothman came to be. Initially, people thought it might be an extraterrestrial being. Back in the 1960s, people were fascinated with UFOs and the possibility of space aliens coming to Earth. But opinions changed when the TNT Area was discovered to be contaminated with pollutants from an old World War II ammunitions factory. People began to think that the pollution might have created the Mothman.

Point Pleasant's Mothman Museum is a popular tourist destination for people who want to see artifacts related to the legendary cryptid.

Then there are people who believe that a large bird combined with people's superstitions may explain sightings of the Mothman. Large herons and owls can have wingspans several feet wide. Owls, such as the large snowy owl, are nocturnal and their eyes can have a reddish glow to them.

Today, people around Point Pleasant have embraced the idea of the Mothman. There is a museum dedicated to the creature downtown. There is also a Mothman Festival every fall that attracts thousands of tourists. We may never know if the Mothman truly exists, but it continues to inspire people's imaginations.

More Creatures that Foretell Doom

The Mothman isn't the only creature of legend that is said to be an omen of doom. Here are a few other creatures that people believe bring misfortune.

Black Cats

While not a cryptid, black cats have been believed to be connected to witches. This has likely given them a bad reputation, because one common superstition is that it's bad luck if a black cat crosses your path.

Black Dogs

Also called Demon Dogs or Hell Hounds, these large, black dogs are believed to be found around the world. Because of their connection to the devil, they are believed to be omens of death.

Banshees

Banshees are supernatural creatures from Irish and Celtic folklore. They appear as old hags. They are a dreadful sight, but to hear them screaming and wailing is a horrible omen. It means a family member is about to die.

White Lady

The White Lady is believed to be a woman who died a horrible death. There are numerous White Lady legends throughout the world. Some stories say she appears in the house of someone who is about to die.

Likho

Likho comes from Slavic folklore. This creature often appears as an old, one-eyed woman. Likho represents evil and brings misfortune and often death to anyone who crosses its path.

Oni

Oni are large, hulking beasts from Japanese mythology. They appear somewhat like ogres with horns and fangs. Their presence often means that a disaster, like an earthquake or plague, is about to occur.

Glossary

ammunition (am-yuh-NIH-shuhn)—bullets and other objects that can be fired from weapons

bunker (BUHNG-kuhr)—a strongly built room or building set beneath the ground

cantilever bridge (CAN-tih-leev-uhr BRIJ)—a bridge with beams that are only supported on one end

celebrity (sell-EH-bruh-tee)—a famous person

contaminated (kuhn-TA-muh-nay-tuhd)—unfit for use because of contact with a harmful substance

cryptid (KRIP-tihd)—an animal or creature that people have claimed to see but has never been proven to exist

cryptozoologist (krip-tuh-zoh-AH-luh-jist)—someone who searches for evidence of unproven creatures such as the Mothman

expedition (ek-spuh-DIH-shuhn)—a journey made for a specific purpose, such as exploring a new region or looking for something

extraterrestrial (ek-struh-tuh-RESS-tree-uhl)—a life form that comes from outer space

fraud (FRAWD)—someone who cheats or tricks people

hoax (HOHKS)—a trick to make people believe something that is not true

mythical (MITH-ih-kuhl)—imaginary or possibly not real

omen (OH-men)—a sign of something that will happen in the future

polluted (puh-LOOT-ed)—unfit or harmful to living things

proof (PROOF)—facts or evidence that something is true

reliable (rih-LYE-uh-buhl)—trustworthy or dependable

reputation (rep-tuh-TAY-shuhn)—a person's character as judged by other people

skeptical (SKEP-tik-ahl)—unable or unwilling to believe things that other people believe in

surveillance (suhr-VAY-luhnss)—having to do with keeping very close watch on someone, someplace, or something, often secretly

terrain (tuh-RAYN)—the surface of the land

TNT (TEE EN TEE)—a flammable compound that is used as an explosive

venomous (VEN-uhm-us)—having or producing a poison called venom

wingspan (WING-span)—the distance between the tips of a pair of wings when fully open

Other Paths to Explore

>>> At the Mothman Museum, you read about the Men in Black. It says that these secret government agents investigate UFO sightings. Their goal is to keep information about UFOs from the public. Imagine that during your search for the Mothman, you come across some Men in Black. Would you work with them to suppress information? Or would you work against them and tell the world about the Mothman?

>>> The TNT Area is heavily polluted. Chemicals used in the old ammunitions factory have seeped into the water and contaminated the ground. Some people say that this toxic pollution created the Mothman. Imagine that it created another monster. What would the monster look like? Would it have wings or razor-sharp claws? Would it be able to fly or run superfast?

>>> At the end of the Chicago story path, you meet a police officer. The officer does not believe your story about the Mothman. But what if she did, and she asked you to lead a citywide search for the cryptid? As a cryptid expert, how would you help city officials hunt for the Mothman?

Read More

Atwood, Megan. *Mothman in the Moonlight*. North Mankato, MN: Stone Arch Books, 2021.

Bowman, Chris. *The Mothman Sightings*. Minneapolis: Bellwether Media, 2020.

Finn, Peter. *Do Monsters Exist?* New York: Gareth Stevens Publishing, 2023.

Krensky, Stephen. *The Book of Mythical Beasts & Magical Creatures*. New York: DK Publishing, 2020.

Internet Sites

How Stuff Works: Hunting Bigfoot and Other Beasts: Explore the World of Cryptozoology
science.howstuffworks.com/science-vs-myth/strange-creatures/cryptozoology.htm

Mothman Festival
mothmanfestival.com

Mothman Museum
mothmanmuseum.com

About the Author

Blake A. Hoena grew up in central Wisconsin, where he wrote stories about robots conquering the moon and trolls lumbering around the woods behind his parents' house. He now lives in Minnesota and enjoys writing about fun things like history, space aliens, cryptids, and superheroes. Blake has written more than one hundred chapter books and dozens of graphic novels for children.

Other Books in This Series